The Gray Boatman

LINDA STRACHAN

ILLUSTRATED BY LIZ ALGER

Rigby

CONTENTS

Scary Stories

ALLY shivered with delight and hugged her knees. She loved Paul's stories, especially the scary ones.

"It was a dark and murky night on the river. The moon struggled to shine through a deep mist that hung above the water. It was the kind of night that sent you rushing home to a warm fire and a hot drink. But if you happened to be on the Garrick Bridge that night, you might wish that you had gone home after all."

Paul paused in the manner of all good storytellers. Ally peered across the room and met Taylor's eyes. They were gleaming in the darkness, and she knew he was enjoying the feeling of being scared just as much as she was. Paul was Ally's big brother, and she had been listening to his stories ever since she had been old enough to understand them.

"Go on, Paul!" said Taylor. Ally had told him all about Paul's amazing stories.

"Okay," said Paul in a dark, velvety voice. "But this is no ordinary story. The story I am about to tell you has been handed down from person to person for generations. It is the tale of the Gray Boatman."

By the time Paul had finished the story, Ally felt shivers all the way down her spine. She was glad she didn't have to walk home along the river and across the Garrick Bridge, like Taylor did.

But when they looked outside it was a clear, starry night and not at all like the night in the story. And it *was* just a story after all.

Taylor told her not to be silly. "Anyway," he said, "I'm meeting my dad up the road. He's just getting off duty." Taylor's dad was a police officer.

2

The Disappearing Act

THE next morning, Ally met Taylor on the way to school.

"That was a great story, wasn't it?" Taylor said. "My dad said he had heard about the Gray Boatman when he was a boy."

"Do you think the story is true?" Ally asked. "The bit about the Gray Boatman coming back every 50 years to take another passenger?"

"I don't know, Ally," Taylor said as he shook his head. "It might be."

"I'd love to see him," Ally said as she stepped onto the small ferry that took them on the short trip to their school. "But it would be so scary!"

Ally and Taylor lived in the small town of Hamslet. The Garrick River flowed through the middle of the town. It was a working river and it was often quicker to take one of the river boats to go places. Ally and Taylor always took a boat to school.

"Guess what?" Taylor whispered when they were sitting on the boat. "My dad was telling me that he has a new case."

"Does it have something to do with that robbery last week?" Ally asked him.

Taylor nodded. "But there's more to it than that. Promise not to tell anyone?"

Ally's eyes widened. "I promise. What is it?"

Taylor looked around to make sure they weren't overheard. But everyone else on the boat was busy talking.

"You see, it wasn't just one jewelry robbery. There have been several, all around this area."

"Really?" squeaked Ally. Usually nothing exciting happened in Hamslet and even one robbery had the whole town talking. "Do they know who did it?"

Taylor shook his head. "That's the exciting part—no one can figure out how the robbers got away. They just seem to have vanished into thin air!"

3

The Gray Boatman

EARLY the next morning, Taylor went out on his paper route. A sea mist hung cold and damp over the river. It was very thick in places.

Taylor's route took him past the old, empty buildings on the wharf. It had once been a busy dock, but most of the old buildings were now deserted. The river opened out onto the sea, just beyond Hamslet.

The sound of oars on the water got Taylor's attention. It was unusual for anyone to be on this part of the river. He strained his eyes to see through the mist, and made out a dark shape on the water.

Suddenly. Taylor remembered Paul's story about the Gray Boatman. Taylor looked around, but he was all alone. The mist had blanketed all of the usual sounds into an eerie quiet, except for the lapping of the water against the bank.

There it was again.

Taylor heard the sound of oars in the water. He stared through the mist. For a moment it swirled, and he caught a glimpse of a man in a small boat—a man who looked gray and shadowy. The Gray Boatman!

Taylor felt his heart thundering. Part of him was screaming to run for his life, but he was rooted to the spot. He didn't want the Gray Boatman to look his way. He didn't want him to come and claim his last passenger. But Taylor couldn't get his feet to move.

A light wind came up and the mist began to break up. Taylor kept looking for the Gray Boatman even though he was terrified that the Gray Boatman would see him first.

The mist cleared and he searched the river for the boat, but it was gone!

4

Detective Work

TAYLOR still felt scared when he told Ally about it later, on their way to school.

"You're sure you saw him?" she asked. Ally wished she could have been there. Taylor gave her a look. If Ally didn't believe him, no one else would.

"Maybe it was someone else, and by the time the mist cleared, they had rowed away, or got out onto the bank."

Taylor shook his head firmly. "You can see right down the river on both sides there," he said. "You know how steep the banks are. There's nowhere to get off the river until you get past the bridge."

"Let's take my boat down there today after school," Ally suggested. "We can see if there is any way he could have gotten off the river without you seeing him."

It was still light when they rowed Ally's little skiff downriver to the old wharf area. Ally saw that Taylor was right. There was nowhere the Gray Boatman could have left the river without Taylor seeing him. It was a long, straight stretch of water with a high bank on one side. The other bank was lined with the tall brick walls of old warehouses.

Daylight was just beginning to fade, and the evening mist started to sweep in from the sea. "Time we went back," said Taylor. "It's getting late."

Just then, Ally shouted, "Look, Taylor!" She pointed across the water.

Taylor spun around and followed the line of her finger to where the river lapped against the foot of the redbrick warehouse walls.

Taylor had no idea what she was pointing at. Ally jabbed her finger toward the wall. "Look at that, Taylor!"

5

A Secret Tunnel

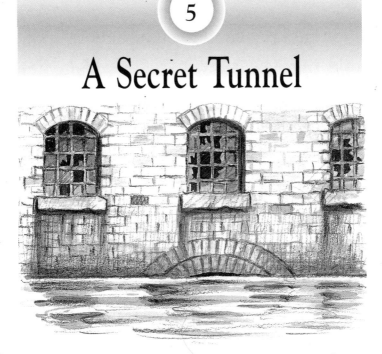

TAYLOR looked at the water rippling against the brick walls, trying to see what Ally had seen. Then he noticed a pattern in the bricks, just at the level of the water. It was hard to see because the rising tide made the river very deep. Twice a day, the Garrick River rose and fell with the tide of the nearby sea. Taylor knew that at this time of day, the tide was almost at its highest point.

"They're the old cellar tunnels," Ally told him, excitedly. "They lead into the loading docks inside the buildings."

Taylor looked at the water that was slowly rising to hide the pattern of bricks.

The bricks had been built into an arch shape, and only the top of the arch was visible—and even that was disappearing fast.

"But the water is almost at the top of the arch. Even when the tide is out there can't be much space under there. How could that have been of any use to anyone?"

"It's not, now," Ally told him. "The river bottom has filled in with mud since the warehouses were in use. That's one of the reasons why people can't get big barges down as far as the Garrick Bridge anymore."

"It's getting dark." Taylor said. "We should go back."

Ally started to turn the little skiff around. "We don't have school tomorrow, so why don't I meet you early in the morning? I could help you get your paper route done faster."

"Great," said Taylor. "Then we'd have enough time to see how low the water is beneath the arches before the tide comes in."

"And we can see if that's where the Gray Boatman went this morning!"

6

Adventure!

ALLY shivered in the chilly morning air. The mist that always seemed to coat the river in the morning was heavy and damp. She and Taylor had delivered all of his papers in double-quick time, and now they were in her little skiff, rowing down the river.

"I feel like the Gray Boatman myself," she said with a giggle.

Even the sound of her voice was different in the heavy air.

"Shhh! And keep closer to the wall, Ally," said Taylor in a hushed whisper.

"Why are you whispering?"

"What if he's here again this morning?" Taylor whispered.

"Who? The Gray Boatman?" Ally tried to shrug off the idea, but somehow in the cold, damp mist, it seemed more difficult to laugh. "I just wish we could see a little better."

Taylor grabbed her arm to stop the oar. He held his finger to his lips. Ally stopped, suddenly scared. She strained her ears for any sounds. The dampening effect of the mist shut out all but the river lapping against the walls.

Taylor shook his head. "Sorry, but I thought I heard something."

"Look, Taylor!" Ally said, pointing.

They had reached the first of the arched cellar openings. They peered in under the arch, but there was only a small space between the water and the top of the arch. It was dark inside.

"We should have brought a flashlight," Taylor said as he pushed the skiff along with his hand flat on the wall. "This arch is too shallow, but there's another one over there."

The next arch was much higher above the water. Ally grabbed the edge of the bricks to hold the skiff steady.

"It's big enough to get inside, Taylor," she whispered.

Voices on the River

"I DON'T know," Taylor frowned. "What if the tide comes in and we get trapped!"

"I checked the times of the tides last night." Ally looked at her watch. "We have almost an hour before the tide comes in again."

"OK, then," Taylor agreed reluctantly. "But let's not go too far in. If the arch tunnel goes too far, we'll come back another time with a flashlight."

Ally nodded. Trust Taylor to be so sensible!

"I'll go first," she said. She turned the little skiff until it was pointing into the tunnel. It was really dark inside. Putting her hands on the roof, Ally started to draw them further into the tunnel.

Suddenly she shrieked. "Taylor! There's a rope here!"

"Where?"

"On the roof of the tunnel. You'll feel it in a minute. It makes it much easier to pull the skiff along."

"Found it!" Taylor felt the rope. It had been fastened to the roof of the tunnel. It was damp and felt slimy in his hand but it was strong and thick. Lying on their backs in the skiff, they were able to pull themselves along quickly.

Taylor was getting used to the dark, and he realized that he could see further along the tunnel. Just then Ally whispered loudly, "Look, Taylor! There's a light up ahead."

Taylor pulled harder on the rope, and in a few minutes they came out of the tunnel. It opened into a large cavern.

Steps led from below the water up to a landing area on their right. All kinds of rusty machinery towered over the waterway.

Ally rowed the skiff toward the landing area, and they climbed out.

"This must be where they unloaded the barges," Ally said, excitedly.

Suddenly, they both heard a noise.

"What's that?" whispered Ally.

"Voices on the river." Taylor's face paled. "I think they're coming down the tunnel!"

8

Danger!

ALLY searched the landing for some-where to hide. There were steps leading up from the back of the landing area, but it would take too long to climb them.

"Quickly," she whispered. "Behind this machine!"

Taylor followed her behind an old rusty crane. They were well hidden by the crane's bulk, but they couldn't see the tunnel.

The voices were whispering. They were getting closer, but the sound of the water in front of their boat made it impossible to hear more than a muttering of words.

"Do you think it's him?" Ally mouthed to Taylor. "The Gray Boatman?"

Taylor stared back open-eyed, as he considered coming face-to-face with the boatman. He heard the whispering coming closer. He put his finger to his lips. They would be discovered if they made a sound.

Taylor was holding his breath. He was sure that the Gray Boatman would hear his heart thundering.

"Throw me the rope!" said a harsh voice.

"Make it quick," said a second voice, much lighter than the first. "Hey! What's that doing there?"

Ally screwed up her face as she remembered the little skiff. They had left it next to the landing. She saw that Taylor was trying to tell her something.

"It's not the Gray Boatman!" he mouthed carefully.

Ally suddenly realized that Taylor was right. She had to get a closer look. There was a gap under the machine just big enough to see through. Ally got down on the ground and peered through.

Two men were examining her little skiff. They were dressed in dark scruffy clothes, and one of them had a hooded jacket. Ally realized that he must have been the one Taylor had seen the day before.

One of the men looked around the landing as if he expected to see someone standing there.

9

Mystery Solved

"THEY must have gone up there!" one of the men said as he jerked his thumb toward the steps. The two men ran for the steps and started to climb them. Ally and Taylor scrambled around the machine to stay out of sight.

As the two men disappeared up the steps, Taylor rushed over to the boat in which the men had arrived.

"Who are they?" Ally asked him.

"I think I know," Taylor said, grabbing a dark cloth from the bottom of the boat.

He held it up and put his hand inside it. Ally stared at it. It had holes in it—two for eyes and, below that, one for a mouth.

"When I realized that it wasn't the Gray Boatman I had seen, I knew it had to be the jewel thieves. This is where they've hidden the loot!"

"Of course!" Ally picked up the other black hood from the boat. "That's how they disappeared! They slipped into the boat and waited for low tide."

"And if anyone saw them, they would think it was the Gray Boatman!" Taylor said, grinning.

Just then, one of the men appeared at the top of the steps. He yelled at the top of his voice, "They're here!"

Ally and Taylor spun around in horror. The two men were running down the steps toward them.

Taylor grabbed Ally's arm. "Get into the boat!" he yelled, pushing her toward the skiff.

Ally needed no urging. She ran to the skiff and leaped into it. The little boat rocked. She held onto the landing to steady it for Taylor. But when she looked up, he wasn't there.

39

The two men were almost at the foot of the steps. Taylor was pushing the men's boat away from the landing toward the tunnel.

"Taylor! Hurry!" she yelled.

Ally got the oar out, but all she could think of was the two men who were now racing toward the landing.

10

The Best Story Ever!

AT LAST, Taylor grabbed the skiff and shoved it as hard as he could toward the tunnel, jumping in as he pushed. The two men were not far behind him.

"Row, Ally!" he shouted. But Ally was already rowing the little skiff toward the tunnel with all her might. The tide was coming in fast and the water was getting close to the roof of the tunnel. Ahead, the men's boat had already disappeared.

They both grabbed the rope and pulled themselves at a racing pace through the tunnel. Ally heard the men shouting as they realized the two were getting away.

There was a splash as one of them jumped into the water. Ally glanced back as she heard the man swim closer. They were almost out of the tunnel.

"Pull harder!" she yelled to Taylor.

Then they were out into the river. Taylor saw the man reach the edge of the tunnel, but he could never catch them now.

"We've got to get the police," said Taylor. He took a turn with the oar and headed toward town.

"But they'll get away before the police come!" Ally said.

Taylor shook his head. "The other man will be stuck in there until the tide goes out. Look how high the water is now!"

Ally looked back. The water was almost at the top of the tunnel, but there was no sign of the man who had been swimming after them.

By the time the tide turned again, the police were waiting outside the tunnel.

Taylor's dad told them later that all the jewels had been recovered and the man who had been swimming was caught before he got to the next town.

The jewelers whose stores had been robbed held a big party for Taylor and Ally.

"And to think it all started with the Gray Boatman," said Ally.

Taylor grinned. "It's still the best, scariest story I've ever heard."